I0626031

SANITY TEST

by

K. E. Adamus

Copyright © 2025 K. E. Adamus

All rights reserved.

2025

161 DAYS

Email: From hubert.l'awl'a@... to w.pawsl'i@...

Dear Doctor,

I would like to kindly inform you that I have not been receiving treatment at your clinic, nor anywhere else, for the past year. The compulsory hospitalization you once promised me in such a case has not been enforced.

I roam free and, from the start, have only been taking half of the massive dose of medication you prescribed me. Thanks to this, I have managed to stockpile several months' worth of supplies.

You are probably wondering why I am writing to you. Well, from my brief observations during my two stays in your hospital, I have concluded that your despotic nature, with its tendency toward eccentricity, strongly resembles that of my recently deceased aunt—the late Pelagia Mróz.

Her funeral took place last week, but I did not attend, as the voices I hear often make me laugh. You, too, would surely agree that giggling at a funeral is inappropriate given the time and occasion.

The reading of the will seemed like a more favorable occasion, especially since my aunt was well aware of my condition—what you call paranoid schizophrenia—and throughout her life, she never held much affection for me. Perhaps it was because, in her opinion, I was too thin for her taste.

I just stepped away from writing this letter to book a ticket to Paris and buy my favorite tea. And what happened?

Hackers—likely working for some government agency, though I have yet to determine which country—prevented me from making the purchase.

They feel untouchable, tormenting a paranoid person, because no one would ever believe such nonsense.

I'll spare you the details and unfortunately won't paint a vivid picture of the mental torment I inflicted upon them in my mind—hopefully also in real life in the future—since such descriptions are not in my interest at the moment.

Let's get back to my aunt.

I was secretly hoping for some cooperation from the voices, expecting that at just the right moment during the reading of the will, they would supply me with some venomous punchline—just as they had on occasion when I sat alone, wasting time thinking.

But the will that was read out silenced even them.

The apartment went to a nephew who has been living in the United States for fifteen years and, as far as I remember, used to regularly pee into my aunt's ferns. The books signed by various authors—books my aunt had traveled far and wide to collect—were given to her niece, who once burned a hole in the deceased's carpet. The oil paintings and watercolors by well-known Polish painters—whose names have long since been lost in my already overly cluttered memory—went to an uncle who, during his first and last trip as an adult, lost his leg with the assistance of a crocodile from the Wrocław Zoo and half a liter of vodka consumed before that fateful encounter with a large reptile.

The details of this intriguing confrontation remain shrouded in family mystery.

The rest of the family received nothing, while I was given the part of the inheritance that requires great responsibility.

Please, doctor, be honest—do you consider me a responsible person? And if not, would you be willing to take possession of my share of the inheritance?

I will include a detailed instruction manual with it.

Best regards, and I wish you an enjoyable time treating lunatics.

Hubert Kawka

Email: From w.pawsľi@... to hubert.ľawľa@...

Dear Patient,

I am concerned about your health. The impulsive decision to give away your inheritance does not reflect well on your mental state. Moreover, this could serve as grounds for filing a petition for your incapacitation and the appointment of a legal guardian.

It is good that you are taking your medication, though unfortunate that you are only taking half the prescribed dose.

Please contact a doctor.

W. Pawski

Email: From hubert.ʳawlʳa@... to w.pawslʳi@...

Dear Doctor,

I doubt whether mere mortals can help me. I believe I have crossed paths with some higher power, and I even know when it happened.

When I was 17, I decided not to believe in God or any supernatural force, and instead, I chose to believe in myself. Perhaps this occurred because none of my prayers were answered, but in any case, from that moment, I began to experience failures. I only realize this now, because at the time, I thought I was succeeding. In hindsight, those moments turned out to be just more stepping stones toward my downfall and complete self-destruction.

I prefer not to discuss the ways in which this looming fate manifests itself at the moment; I don't think it serves my interests. I will only say that these are imponderables because I still suspect the secret services of being involved in the mysterious disappearance of objects. I plan to ignore this fate or higher power.

I believe that excessive interest in my person reflects advanced foolishness. This is probably how I concluded that God is foolish, and remembering my own actions—those I'm too ashamed to mention, but which attest to my idiocy—I began to feel equal to God.

I hope this email doesn't fall into the hands of religious fanatics, because I think my situation would be even worse than it is now—so far, I only occasionally inspect the rooftops for snipers aiming at me.

Returning to more earthly matters—my aunt gave me a dog as a gift.

It's a crossbreed between a chow-chow and a dachshund.
  Chow-chow doesn't refer to the sounds dogs make, but to a breed, though I don't know how to spell the name.
  I haven't seen the beast yet, but I've already heard quite a bit from my cousin, who is taking care of it until the inheritance is passed on to me—unfortunately.

I think the dog could use a miniature safety straitjacket (a version for four legs) and some proper therapy, which is why I thought of you.

Best regards,
Hubert Kawka

Email: From w.pawsl′i@... to hubert.l′awl′a@...

Dear Patient,

As far as I know, although I am not particularly religious, God is said to care for everyone, so you shouldn't feel overly special or fall into a delusion of grandeur.

As your doctor, I shouldn't be writing such a biting statement, but I must admit, you are getting on my nerves.

Your letter suggests advanced psychosis. Please contact a doctor.

W. Pawski

P.S. I doubt the dog exists.

Email: From hubert.l′awl′a@... to w.pawsl′i@...

Dear Doctor,

Apparently, the dog does exist. I myself doubted that such a creature could walk this Earth after reading just a few of the messages from my cousin, and I've already received several hundred. As you can probably guess, the situation is urgent.

So far, you haven't replied to me about whether you agree to take on the dog. I probably forgot to mention that I am giving it away completely for free. I can also throw in a copy of the book I plan to finish in a few months.

I await your definitive response.

Best regards,
Hubert Kawka

Email: From   gocureyourself@...   to hubert.l′awl′a@...

Annoying Patient,

I'm writing this email from a new account on purpose. I want to tell you what I think about your attempt to write a book; yes, I've had enough of your emails.

The very idea of writing a book is fundamentally noble, but I must warn you that this attempt will end in failure. In a word—nobody will buy your book because, judging by your emails, nothing will make sense, it won't hold together, and there will certainly be chaos and lawlessness reigning instead.

In short, you will just waste your time, which you probably don't have much of, as most schizophrenics don't live to an old age.

Please use that time for something productive, and if you can't, at least don't harm society, like by distracting me from my work.

An Angry Doctor

Email: From hubert.lʳawlʳa@... to w.pawslʳi@...

Dear Doctor,

It is with regret that I must inform you that I found a logical error in your statement. It's in the following sentence:
  "There will certainly be chaos and lawlessness reigning."

I believe these are contradictory states. Since you have already made an opinion (though, I should add, without having read a single page of my book) that *"chaos will reign"* in my novel, why did you also mention a state of *"lawlessness"*?

I think you might be confused with your terminology; your profession has probably caused some involuntary brainwashing.

"*Lawlessness*" refers to a state of no rule, and you yourself stated that *"chaos will rule."*

It's an odd choice, perhaps you were trying for some sort of personification?

But then again, you're a psychiatrist, so I shouldn't be too surprised.

As for the sales of my book, I'm counting on the other schizophrenics. I'm not sure how many people there are in the world right now, but 3% of that is quite a significant target group.

Please don't worry about the marketing; I plan to profit from my illness.

Best regards,
Hubert Kawka

Email: From graphomaniarules@... to hubert.lawla@...

Annoying Patient,

I'm writing from yet another account because you've pushed me to my limit. You must be practicing your retorts on yourself due to lack of contact with other people—no one likes schizophrenics, and there are reasons for that. I'll spare you those reasons out of mercy.

Do you think you are the only one being followed, or are others too?
 And can you tell me why anyone would waste their time and money tracking you? You're not the Minister of Economy, and your writing attempts are probably embarrassing.

Paparazzi have to be earned.

Please take your medication and contact a doctor.

Former Doctor

P.S. Please don't come to my clinic.

Email: From hubert.ľawľa@... to w.pawsľi@...

Dear Doctor,

There are many reasons for someone to be watching me. The first, chronologically... Maybe it's better if I mention the second... It's as follows: before my first stay in the hospital, I managed to escape from the police station. I don't think this happens often among detainees, so it could have been one of the reasons for surveillance. To me, it's a trivial reason, but no one understands the logic of thinking of so-called "mentally healthy" people.

Experience has taught me that so-called "normal" people are more unpredictable than madmen. I'm more afraid of madmen, but at least the fact that they might snap has a high probability, whereas in the case of healthy people, it's always an unpleasant surprise.

After long reflection, I must conclude that I have yet to meet a person whose mind is in perfect order. The most common affliction among the people I've encountered is neurosis.
I've noticed some signs of it in you.

If you don't want to follow the path of your nurses, who secretly swallow pills from the hospital pharmacy, I suggest you start drinking lemon balm tea.

Sincerely concerned about the state of your nerves,
 Hubert Kawka

Email: From hubert.l′awl′a@... to w.pawsl′i@...

Dear Doctor,

How is your herd doing on the locked ward?

What I'm about to write may sound like the ramblings of a sick lunatic, but I feel I have a mission to fulfill.

I imagine you're now thinking this is something like finding a lost dagger of a porcelain dynasty and then using it to kill the president.

You are mistaken.

First and foremost, I abhor violence and definitely prefer healthy interpersonal interactions, which are rather rare in today's reality. The mission is a difficult task.

It is about changing the way schizophrenics are perceived and granting them the benefit of the doubt. Currently, schizophrenia means the depreciation of the testimony of someone suffering from it in court.

I'm asking myself, am I the only one being followed by unknown organizations (the fact that it's a team of people indicates they have a large sum of money, leading to the conclusion that it's some kind of government organization).

There are a few possible explanations. Either those who are being watched are the more intelligent ones, or perhaps scientific studies are being conducted on them, though I hope they are not experiments. It sounds paranoid, but for certain agencies, paranoia could be an interesting phenomenon. They might be conducting research on how to stir it into a manic state, and then use the acquired knowledge to induce a few days of diarrhea in someone like Gaddafi.

Whatever motivates these organizations, their actions are unpunished, because the facts presented by schizophrenics sound like a summary of a thriller or action movie, and psychiatrists who listen to these outpourings have closed minds.

I realize how bizarre my words sound; yes, I've already seen many expressions portraying embarrassment, pity, or horror that someone could be this insane.

So, this mission is doomed to failure, but I feel I have the potential to stir up some chaos in this world.

Please don't ask me whether I take medication. I always hear that question when I tell stories that actually happened to me, and it's starting to annoy me.

P.S. I'm sending the dog. Apparently, it doesn't exist, so there's nothing for you to worry about.

Email: From hubert.l⁄awl⁄a@... to w.pawsl⁄i@...

Dear Doctor,

Judging by your silence, it seems the dog hasn't yet reached its destination. Recently, I heard about an emergency landing of a plane, during which a dog bit a stewardess and several passengers. The breed doesn't quite match, but I think no one would disclose the true genealogy of the Curator, as it would tarnish the airline's reputation.

I know, I know, the Curator was supposed to reach you by land, but given the nature of this dog, it may be a long and tiresome journey for those around him.

Please let me know when the dog finally arrives at your place. I prefer not to inquire about it myself. The shipment was sent using the personal details of the mayor of Dungs.

Isn't the name of the town picturesque? Any complaints will need to be addressed to the mayor.

I imagine you're outraged, but what did you expect from a madman? You yourselves opened the door for us by labeling us as insane, illogical, and irrational.

By the way, I think that using someone else's personal data in this case was entirely rational. Oh right, I forgot that the dog is a product of my imagination, but I think that after seeing this creature, you'll believe in aliens.
 You probably think of me as a cold psychopath who doesn't care about the fate of even imaginary animals. Well, I do care, hence my

letters. I would actually worry about the dog's fate. Doctors are soulless, and Kustosz would surely end up as a lab rat if not for his lucky dog star, which many people who have encountered this dog would want to eliminate.

And now, a question from a different angle. Sometimes, I catch myself in a dream composing sentences for my novel, and their quality exceeds everything I am able to create while awake. I wake up thinking that I have created something magnificent, but unfortunately, I remember nothing, and instead of those sublime sentences, all that comes out of my mouth is the mundane: "fuck!"
 What do you think about that? I hope you'll rise above the psychiatric swearing and give me some interesting feedback.

Regards,
Hubert Kawka

Email: from w.pawsl'i@... to leon.l'rol@...

Dear Sir,

I am the head of the closed ward at the psychiatric hospital in Bows.

I am writing to you out of concern for your safety.

For some time now, I have been receiving emails from one of my former patients. It is unknown where he is currently located, but judging by the content of his letters, he is in a state of acute psychosis and is not taking his medication.

In one of his emails, he mentioned that he started using your personal data. I will not overwhelm you with medical terminology to analyze this behavior. I will simply say that he is a dangerous individual, endowed with a certain perverse intelligence that prevents him from functioning normally in society, but it may facilitate the commission of crimes that are difficult to carry out.

The patient's name is Hubert Kawka.

Unfortunately, I do not remember what he looks like; I do not actually recall this case at all, which should influence your caution – these inconspicuous types are the most dangerous.

Please take care of your safety and the safety of your family, if you have one.

Best regards,
Włodzimierz Pawski

Email: from getlost@... to hubert.rawra@...

Sick mind!

I didn't want to inform you about this earlier, due to unnecessary delicacy in this case, but I absolutely cannot recall your case.

Since your psychiatrist doesn't remember it, how is it possible that *They* have become interested in you and still remember you? Well, *Unremembered Case* – this is impossible.

Please visit the nearest psychiatric clinic, schedule an appointment, buy your medication, and start taking it. I am not writing this out of concern for your insignificant person, but out of concern for society, which is forced to interact with you, meaning – your family, which is probably supporting you.

Unfortunately, no one has yet invented a cure for megalomania – I think you need such medication.

My experience with your signs of psychosis, in the form of emails to a doctor, has led me to increase the medication dosage for all patients with unclear personalities, whom I had not previously paid special attention to.

I hope I haven't developed an allergy to mediocrity in the process.

A rational doctor

Email: From hubert.l'awl'a@... to w.pawsl'i@...

Nervous doctor!
Not wanting to worsen your stomach upset, I will focus on a neutral topic for us, which is money. Just like you, with my modest contribution (as you can see, I'm not falling into megalomania, I'm just stating the facts), have developed an allergy to mediocrity, I, unfortunately, suffer from a financial allergy. Apparently, I cannot bear the thought of becoming wealthy. I cannot become wealthy because of thoughts about hackers.
Why keep money in an account when it can be stolen at any moment? Why keep money at home, where it can be even easier to take? I have my own evidence of the presence of hackers and burglars, but, due to your reserve, I will leave it out.
However, hackers are a false lead. The source of my financial allergy lies within my psyche.
Yes, I wanted to lead you astray and it brought me joy. After all, I am not normal and teasing others brings me pleasure, even more so because it's something I can't share with anyone.
But let me proceed to describe the allergy. It looks something like this:

I slowly gather and save money.
When the amount reaches a few thousand, I

catch the flu.

I respect myself, and when I have a few thousand in my account and I'm sick, I don't go to work, even though I know the bastards won't pay me.

I turn on my laptop, patiently close virus warnings, and start buying things I've wanted to buy for years, or things I've never thought of, with exclamations like: *Oh, screw it!*

And that's when controlled shopping addiction sets in – I spend all my money down to the amount necessary to cover living costs until the next paycheck.

I go to bed broke, go to some party the next day, drink alcohol, wake up with a moral hangover, and then the anxiety of bankruptcy emerges.

To drown out the conscience of a shopaholic, I start working on my personal development (yes, that should scare you), which is such a thankless task that it allows me to effectively forget about the miserable amount in my account.

In the meantime, I get better and go back to working at the factory.

I have – according to you, unjustified – the suspicion that if I just wanted to and weren't so lazy, I would be higher up the social ladder. I didn't feel like it.

This proves my mediocrity, which is why I'm not offended by your previous email.

Please analyze my financial allergy. I think it could be an interesting intellectual exercise, as long as you enjoy such games.

Sincerely, The Annoying Patient

Email: From: leon.krol@... To: w.pawski@...

Murderer!

I knew you weren't right in the head the moment I happened to assist with your job interview, assuming you're Wlodzimierz Padaczkowski.

If you are him, the destruction of the forestry school and the death of the mushroom picker are on your conscience.

But if you're Hubert Kawka, the one you supposedly warned me about, I heard about your discharge from the hospital, and after reading this letter, we'll prepare for your "return." Don't count on mercy.

This entire letter reeks of psychosis. You have the audacity to impersonate a psychiatrist to scare us? Mushroom pickers have started learning English because apparently, you ran away abroad, if you're Włodek.

I'm treating this letter as a criminal threat and am passing the matter to the police.

Leon Król
PS Is Bows named after that bow from which you killed Mietek, you asshole?

Email: From w.pawsl'i@... to hubert.l'awl'a@...

Yes, this time you actually managed to fool me. Is the mayor of Dungs an acquaintance from the psychiatric hospital? From what I know, such acquaintances don't last long, and most likely, the mayor wouldn't keep in touch with you.
You probably memorized his name and surname and obtained his address by some means known only to you.

I am keeping my promise—especially since impersonating another person is a criminal offense—and I am filing a request in court for a mandatory treatment order. I am a serious person, and the ocean of my psychiatric patience has been exhausted.

Let me add that I am doing this for your own good. It's a waste of time to let your life be consumed by illness. In the hospital, you'll have plenty of time to write your book, and you'll be able to test direct marketing strategies on your target audience.

Here's a suggestion: try expanding your market to people suffering from depression. I think your ramblings might actually cheer them up.

See you in a straitjacket.

Doctor

Email: From hubert.l'awl'a@... to w.pawsl'i@...

Dear Doctor,

I am fully aware that I am mentally ill, yet I still believe that understanding your letter would be difficult even for a normal person.

I chose the mayor of Dungs as the donor of personal data completely at random. While browsing a map of Poland, I came across the town of Dungs, and its charming name stuck in my memory. Sometimes I wondered what it would be like to be one of its residents. So when I was forced to use someone's details, I didn't hesitate for long. However, I am lazy and didn't check online to see what the mayor's actual name is. Could it be that the name I provided coincidentally matches reality? Hmm. Let's think about this for a moment.

If you had seen the sender's address written on the crate with the dog, that would mean you had already encountered that Gremlin—as my cousin called him. Yet, you don't mention this unfortunate animal at all.

This suggests that the story about the mayor must be quite interesting. Please fill me in on the details and let me know—did the dog finally reach you?

Intrigued patient, aka coincidence hunter

P.S. Thank you for the suggestion regarding the new target group. I must admit that I have some trouble with self-discipline when it comes to writing my book.

In 2010, I only managed to write 20 pages. (If this continues at the same pace, days will have 52 hours, and my future reincarnations will still be struggling with the novel. I don't believe in reincarnation, though :p)

In my search for materials for self-administered brainwashing (i.e., to find motivation), I started browsing the internet and came across numerous groups of success fanatics. I think my stories about life's losers could serve as a perfect illustration of the starting point of a millionaire's career—the shoeshine boy stage.

Perhaps one day, I'll start writing e-books for them under a pseudonym. One of those books might accidentally find its way to you, and in this incidental way, a patient will end up brainwashing the doctor.

Telegram
Police Station in Dungs to Police Station in Bows

Please conduct an interview with Wlodzimierz Pawski. On January 6, 2011, we received a request from the mayor of Dungs Municipality to verify the identity of Wlodzimierz Padaczkowski, who claims to be a psychiatrist at the psychiatric hospital in Bows.

There is reason to suspect that he is not who he claims to be. The request is attached.

Senior Sergeant Jacek Klimuszko, Criminal Division, Police Station in Dungs

Official Letter:
Police Station in Bows to Wlodzimierz Pawski

Notification

Please report to the Police Station in Bows on January 13, 2011, at 11:30 AM in Room No. 6 to provide testimony.

Sergeant Magda Wojtyla
Criminal Division, Police Station in Bows

26/28 Forrester Street, Bows

Email: From w.pawsl'i@... to hubert.l'awl'a@...

Wanted Menace,

During my accidental visit to the local police station, I submitted a request to locate your infuriating person and subject you to involuntary treatment. After reviewing the case, the police will forward the proceedings to the court.

This will undoubtedly happen automatically—harassing me with stupid emails and identity theft are sufficient grounds to get you locked up for the next six months. I hope you end up in a different ward than mine; I have no desire to see your utterly unmemorable face.

Adieu!

Email: From hubert.l′awl′a@... to w.pawsl′i@...

Dear Doctor,

You cannot accuse me of identity theft—I checked online—the mayor has a different name than the one written on the dog's crate. Besides, you must admit that I have every right to succumb to delusions of grandeur, considering that, despite your long medical practice, I managed to provoke you to the point of taking the matter to court.

Let's summarize the realities that led you to this decision:

1. Letters from a sad lunatic, full of incoherent reflections
2. A package containing an imaginary dog

Besides, I remember your conditions well—the request for forced treatment was to be submitted to the court in the case of refusing treatment, and you have no proof of that (nor of identity theft, I assume; I bet you deleted all the emails... oops, I just incriminated myself... Włodek, please, delete this email!).

Hubert Kawka

P.S. Where I live, they resist treating me with all their might.
P.S. 2 I am attaching an essay written by a student of my late aunt, who was a teacher. She made him read it aloud to the entire class, and three days later, she was found dead.
P.S. 3 Recently, I met someone from the village of Dungs

Attachment

Essay
"How I Spent My Summer Vacation"
Jan Kowalski, Class II C

My summer vacation was as dull and gray as my personal data. When I was a child, I used to think my last name belonged to some important figure, since I kept seeing it on most mailboxes.

I imagined it belonged to a fearless courier whose speed determined the fate of the world. The truth was disappointing.

Another truth is that I will never become a writer, given that by the second sentence of my essay, I have already drifted into a digression. So, let's return to my unfortunate summer break.

Although, here comes another digression—why do teachers have the privilege of peeking into our private time, those two months free from the torment of school? Why have we never heard about *their* vacations? Is there some kind of censorship surrounding these stories?

I quickly return to the topic, as I can already sense a brilliant thought forming in my teacher's mind about giving me a failing grade. Yes, I feel that I could have made a career as Nostradamus—if not for my painfully common name.

I spent my summer working in a fruit and vegetable processing plant, under the watchful eye of a supervisor named *Wojna* ("War"). Judging by her character, her ancestors must have engaged in highly combative activities—whether in neighborhood battles over 20 centimeters of disputed land or in world wars where their mere existence surely contributed to many victorious battles, perhaps even leading to Hitler's downfall.

Life in the factory revolved around breaking records in the speed of stuffing cucumbers into jars. Due to my natural precision, I did not participate in this rat race, which meant I didn't earn much. However, my jars were used as models to show the other workers how a properly packed jar should look. *Wojna* would pause her work and proudly parade them around the entire factory floor.

After about a month and a half, the cucumber supply ran out, and I was left in idleness. I had plenty of time to think, which—combined with my age—could only lead to bad decisions. I decided to hitchhike to the mountains.

The trip was supposed to last a week, but on the first night, I had a close encounter with a mother bear and quickly abandoned my plans. I returned home, covered in mud.

After this humiliating defeat, I spent the rest of my vacation at home, silently protesting the good weather.

Email: From w.pawsl′i@... to hubert.l′awl′a@...

Strange patient!

A package with a dog has arrived for me. Considering its prolonged stay in an animal crate, it displayed unexpected vitality and smelled of designer perfume.
 Out of pity for the animal, I took it for a walk.

The dog led me straight to the nearest museum and urinated on its door in full view of the city guards. I had to pay a fine.

However, I am not one of those misers who would start insulting someone just because of lost money. In fact, I have far more reasons to insult you.

I smell a serious conspiracy here. Let's start with some questions:

How did the dog, named Curator, know where the nearest museum was?

Why did it urinate only on its doors, when there were plenty of other, much more suitable objects along the way, according to canine customs?

This suggests a hypothesis: the dog was trained.
 Which means that for a certain period, you

regularly walked the dog from my house to the museum.

This, in turn, indicates that you suffer from a severe psychosis and pose a threat to me and the rest of society.

I have informed the police.

The officers reviewed the personal data of patients in my clinic and the hospital where I work. They found no record of anyone named Hubert Kawka.

They decided to check the CCTV footage from the museum, but this seems like a Sisyphean task since it's unclear exactly when you trained the dog.

Please voluntarily report to the nearest psychiatric clinic and submit to treatment.

Soon, you will be tracked down by the IP address from your computer, from which the emails were sent.

Wlodzimierz Pawski

Email: From hubert.l′awl′a@... to w.pawsl′i@...

Oh crap, I completely forgot about you and the dog, and it's already almost a year since the last email. In my defense, I've been working two jobs, but still, I feel terrible for forgetting about that poor animal.
Let me explain everything step by step:

I never trained the dog, because I've never even seen it. After I inherited the dog, my cousin took care of it in my place, and he can vouch for my honesty in this matter.

The dog was named Curator because of its behavior – peeing on museum doors. No one could explain how it finds museum buildings or why it urinates on them.
As someone who's not entirely of sound mind, I'll suggest two hypotheses:

The dog is the reincarnation of a crazy museum curator.

The dog is a type of conqueror, relieving its canine complexes by territorial marking what has not yet been marked by other dogs.
Honestly, I don't know what this is all about.

Thirdly (back to explaining your theories and hypotheses) – I've been treated twice in your hospital, and I have no idea why my personal data disappeared from the records of this serious institution.

Fourth – I am trying to get treatment, but the local psychiatrists are reluctant to help. I should add that, in my objective opinion, they themselves are in need of psychiatric care.

I also read my nonsense, that is, the emails, and I must admit that they don't point to a common-sense type of thinking from their author.

(By the way, I apologize for the typos in the emails, but my computer was hacked, which is why, for example, the small "i" changes to an uppercase I. And of course, the quotation marks turned out nicely as small, to contradict my words.)

I also abandoned my mission of changing the way people think about other schizophrenics, because I have no intention of taking responsibility for their potential actions after giving them the benefit of the doubt and trust. I don't want to fall into a grandiose delusion, but I'm probably one of the few schizophrenics who, despite their illness, can function normally in society without being suspected of any mental illness.

I should add that I do not belong to the so-called "forgotten cases." In every environment, I function like a celebrity – my behavior and my person are the source of general interest and gossip.

I should also note that I am not particularly thrilled with this state of affairs.

The dog was probably noticed by a stewardess, but after a year of battling its habits, she gave up and sent the package again to the intended address.

As far as I know, donations, as an act in themselves, are not punishable. However, as far as I remember, the police were supposed to deal with my case earlier, but that never happened.

How do you explain this?

Best regards,

Hubert Kawka

Email: From w.pawsl′i@... to hubert.l′awl′a@...

I just realized how inappropriate it was to contact you. You will probably flood me with emails about close encounters of the first degree with aliens working for the CIA, or shapeshifters disguised as mixed-breed dogs.

Then, you will likely go on about coincidences that a healthy person wouldn't even notice, but in your consciousness, distorted by a serious mental illness, these will be arguments forming the foundation of bizarre conspiracy theories, where the main roles will be played by reincarnations of prominent historical figures who simply cannot find eternal rest until they contact you.

I would like to point out that this was irony, not a confirmation of facts, although I'm sure you will perceive the current statement as smoke and mirrors, as all direct information is at risk of being intercepted by "them."

Out of pure scientific curiosity, may I ask who "they" are according to you? Have you already figured out the nationality of your persecutors and the name of the powerful state organization they belong to?

Wishing you mental health and a return to reality,
W.P.

Email: From hubert.ŕawlŕa@... to w.pawslŕi@...

I think I am being persecuted by the descendants of the Great Frog, to whom no one has ever prayed, which has caused its megalomania to be encoded in the genetic code, resulting in superintelligent, talking frogs. They do not communicate with just anyone, as can be traced in the collective consciousness. Legends only mention their contacts with representatives of royal families.

Based on this data, I dare to claim that I am a descendant of some illegitimate line leading to the peak of the world's power, and the frogs are persecuting me to remember my heritage. When I am on top, I must weave the image of the Great Frog into my crown

Analyzing my previous statements as an anthropologist, I would see the Great Frog as a symbol of an international plague.
Currently, I dare say, power is based in part on access to information (for example, regarding advanced technologies).

The plague, therefore, would be misinformation, and I am it's sower. Our worldview is also based on information.

Let's imagine that due to new evidence, we must question our previous perception of the world. Individual cogs in the social machine would cease to function properly.

Have I led you astray already? Do you believe in the theory of the Great Frog?

Sincerely,
Hubert Kawka

P.S.
Have I perhaps found a way to a "mental" revolution?

I should add that the arguments in this email were made up on the spot (yes, I'm a bit creative), to mock you, just as you like to do with your patients.

I still don't know who my persecutors are, but I hate them for their annoying attempts to destroy my life and psyche.

I'll spare you the examples of their negative and unlawful activities, as I realize how improbable they sound.

I will finally get to work on my own failure, make money for the lawsuits, and put things in order with them. Or maybe I'll have some fun with them, using their methods, and then it might not be so funny anymore.

Email: From w.pawsl′i@... to hubert.l′awl′a@...

I must admit, you are somewhat original in your illness. But my scientific interest will not prevent me from contacting the authorities.

Currently, I am preparing materials for an international conference, so I am a bit too busy to visit the police station. I have indeed never heard of the theory of the Great Frog.

However, I must reveal to you that any changes in human mentality are the result of a long and tedious process, due to our conservative nature.

Therefore, I do not foresee a bright revolutionary career for you. Your theory of the Great Frog would amuse me, were it not for your readiness to turn the established order upside down.

And please tell me, how on earth did you manage to finish your studies? Did you pretend to be sane? Or did no one bother to read your surely bizarre thesis?

It is certainly a huge success, but I think the university staff were informed about your illness,

and out of pity gave you the diploma, fully aware that you would not find a job in any normal position.
What is your current line of work? Still honing your skills in a factory?

WP

Email: From hubert.l⁄awl⁄a@... to w.pawsl⁄i@...

Certainly, my current profession will terrify you. I am a security guard in England. In my job, dealing with Batman is an everyday occurrence. However, unlike in cartoons and movies, I am able to convince him to take off his mask. Yes, you probably just thought: "If you throw a stone into a pack of dogs, the one that gets hit will bark."

So, let me explain — Batman is a teenager who went to a pub where I worked, dressed as Batman.
I believe my job is to practice the art of diplomacy. On my very first day in this profession, I decided to be polite to customers, putting myself in their shoes. Let's imagine someone is heading somewhere — a pub, a theater, a concert. Usually, they are motivated by the need for social interaction and a desire for acceptance. So, if the

staff treats them like crap, they may feel a bit down.

That's why I try to be friendly and polite to everyone. If someone doesn't respond to that, I give a command in an even more polite manner, and in most cases, the person's shoulders slump, and they realize they've reached a dead end.
Of course, all these rules do not apply to troublesome idiots, who are shown the door and banned for life from the premises.

I've also noticed a few interesting things in this job. Even though I don't drink any alcohol while working at a nightclub, by the end of my shift, I feel slightly dizzy, and the next day, I have a hangover.

I explain this to myself as the production of endorphins in the body, due to being in a crowd having fun.

I also conduct sociological research, classifying people into different types of clients.

Besides that, please be careful and don't fall off the toilet, on which, as far as I know, you spend long hours typing on your laptop. I also train in martial arts.

That's all the information about my profession for now.

HK

Email: From w.pawsl′i@… to hubert.l′awl′a@…

Dear patient,

I will try to be nice in this email so that you don't feel particularly bad and go off murdering innocent members of English society.

I do *not* spend long hours on the toilet. That is a slanderous lie, the invention of a certain nurse who developed a pathological obsession with me. Before she was fired, she spread all sorts of gossip about me, to the delight of our mentally unbalanced patients.

Therefore, I categorically deny that:

1. I sit on the toilet with my trousers down and write academic articles in that state.

2. I stand in front of a mirror holding a potted fern saying: "My name is Leon. You don't want to know my surname," repeating this

several times a day.

3. I suffer from insomnia and, when I can't sleep, I go to a phone booth to make prank calls to less favored acquaintances.

4. I torment my neighbors by pounding schnitzels at 8 a.m. on Sundays and mowing the lawn at 6am on Saturdays.

Furthermore:

1. I do *not* torment a cat, as I don't own one.

2. I do *not* administer horse doses of medication out of malice, but because the patients need it.

3. I *can* park and do *not* scratch 30 cars a day due to clumsy attempts at the task.

4. I do *not* run a blog describing the misadventures of friends and patients.

5. I do *not* report people to the police.

6. etc...

You've shown just how little brain power you possess by believing all that nonsense. Despite your master's degree, you clearly lack a scientific way of perceiving the world — especially in the field of everyday reality.

Your mental illness makes you question and ponder the most trivial matters and processes, ones that sane minds don't even notice. A beetle species seen for the first time becomes, in your mind, proof of extraterrestrial origins — especially if it's green. You're constantly assaulted by signs and symbols confirming your delusional theories about how the world works.

Let me reveal a secret: the end of the world is near. Please begin stockpiling water and food. Do not leave your home — if you stray more than 10 meters from it, the end of the world will occur instantly.

You must not communicate in any language other than Polish. If you utter even a single word in a foreign tongue, the end of the world will occur instantly.

Please stop going to work. I've received word that "they" will be waiting for you there.

With kind blessings of prosperity,
WP

Email: From hubert.l'awl'a@... to w.pawsl'i@...

Dear Doctor,

You are right: the end of the world is near.

An acquaintance of mine works at the National Health Fund (NFZ) and has confidentially learned of a new epidemic with epicenters in Africa. This information has not yet reached the press — a phenomenon so rare that it almost confirms the end is near, especially when a Polish schizophrenic knows more than BBC journalists.

This epidemic targets the brain, weakening thinking capacity, structures of perception, analysis, etc. The environment only notices that a given person seems to be plagued by bad luck. Through a string of mistakes, the afflicted lose their jobs. In intimate moments, they call their partners by the wrong names. Chaos creeps into their small daily rituals.

As you can imagine, the illness leads their lives to ruin.

Worse still, it spreads via airborne droplets, like the flu. The incubation period lasts several months. Several cities in Africa have already been infected.

Specialists are still debating what they might be dealing with. Chaos reigns in these cities, resulting from small but systematically committed errors by tens or hundreds of thousands of people.

Drivers are making mistakes. Bankers, judges, shopkeepers too...

One might think crime would surge in such cities — but criminals are plagued by misfortune as well. They're constantly caught by the police. Police officers make errors, the criminals are released, only to discover their lawyers made mistakes too, so the criminals go to prison, where the prison staff also make errors, the criminals escape, but make mistakes again...

I'm so terrified that I've stopped buying bananas and oranges — even though they're imported here from South America and Greece. Somehow, they still remind me of Africa.

Should you notice any of the symptoms described, please report to the NFZ and ask for a certain pill, which is literally called "Certain Pill" (the name derives from its effectiveness). Apparently, this drug works.

Best regards,
H.K.

Email: From w.pawsl'i@... to hubert.l'awl'a@...

Do you take me for an idiot?

I can already imagine your hysterical laughter at the mere thought of me going to the NFZ and asking about *a certain pill* because I've been struck by an epidemic of bad luck... or a certain pill *for* bad luck... or a pill that's called *certain* because I had bad luck...

This could end in one of two ways:

1. I'd be handed the "morning-after" pill

2. I'd be admitted to *my own* hospital as a patient, to the delight of my "herd," as you once so eloquently called my patients —

who would then be free to torment me without consequence...

But what am I even worrying about? An email from a madman? *Pfft.* I'm off to work. You should go to sleep — at least there's a greater chance you won't screw anything up in your dreams.

— Doctor

P.S.
 And are you really going to claim you're *yourself*?

Email: From hubert.lᐟawlᐟa@... to w.pawslᐟi@...

Am I myself? *Ahem.* And which one of my personalities are you referring to?

P.S.
 Attaching the first chapter of my novel. I have a feeling you'll make an invaluable critic.

P.S.2
 Please don't limit your hypotheses to a clearly narrow number — unforeseen circumstances may arise, and then another thing, or several different things, might occur.

P.S.3

Attaching the whole unfinished novel. Awaiting your constructive feedback (I dislike linguistic clichés too).

Email: From w.pawsl'i@... to hubert.l'awl'a@...

I read the first chapter of your novel out of curiosity. That curiosity wasn't driven by the fact that the piece was written by a schizophrenic.

What intrigued me was what a murderer might write. Yes, a murderer.

From sources available to me, I've learned that you have your boss, Marian, on your conscience. I must admit I began reading with a certain apprehension — I've dealt with a few psychopaths in my career, and they certainly didn't make for good drinking buddies.

Your dispassionate, mechanical writing style does not give me good vibes. What do you intend to do to that unfortunate heroine?

Is she a real person, currently decomposing in someone's backyard or a forest — your next victim?

Did you kill your aunt too?

Have you chosen me as your confidant, so the world can learn of your "successes" in killing people?

— W. Pawski

Email: From hubert.ʎawlʎa@... to w.pawslʎi@...

I've also taken the liberty of reading your cheerful literary efforts in the form of your emails, and I must admit — just as the ocean of my stupidity is wide and bottomless, so too has my confusion now reached the depths of the Mariana Trench.

Did you ignore my advice about drinking calming herbal teas and start experimenting with medications from the hospital pharmacy?

I understand my emails may be incoherent, inconsistent, and full of nonsense about Mary's ass flying off in the wind, but from you, I expected something more logical and tethered to reality.

Are mental illnesses contagious? Have you gone mad? Who the hell is Marian?

I don't recall any boss of mine by that name. Do I have a serious (say, years-long) memory gap, and then someone brainwashed me and gave me plastic surgery?

Your email is more terrifying than my graphomania about a gray man without a personality.

Please explain.

— Hubert Kawka

Email: From w.pawsl′i@... to hubert.l′awl′a@...

You don't need brainwashing; you're doing quite well losing your grip on reality.
 Could you be so distracted that you forgot about your past crimes? I'll say upfront, that's not a good defense in court. Maybe you pulled off the schizophrenia trick — you really convincingly pretended to be mentally ill, but amnesia is a whole other level.
 Why didn't you go to acting school and instead used your gift in such a brutal way?
 Contact with you is now even more unpleasant (although a few months ago I could hardly imagine that was possible — back then I thought it couldn't get worse).

Please do not write to me anymore. The police will be contacting you soon.

W.P.

Email: From hubert.ƚawƚa@... to w.pawsƚi@...

I wouldn't write to you anymore, out of respect for others' wishes, but this is really getting intriguing.
 The biggest revelation is that you've started to consider me a sane person.

Other patients would probably mark the day they received such a medical opinion on their calendar, then, communicating online with "other-normal" people, would declare that date the "International Day of Accidental Nutcases."
 A few years ago, I would have been glad to hear that I'm mentally healthy, but now, burdened with strange and unwanted experiences, I sense an unhealthy scandal brewing here, one I definitely don't want to be part of.
 My voices agree with me — one just said:
 "What a sound mind!"
 Damn, are they also against me? Trying to screw me over with their statements?
 I don't yet know what you're trying to frame me for, but I already see how this hypothetical case

ends: "The person is sane. Even the voices they hear confirm it."

Just as I once tried to prove to everyone that my head was okay, now I'll be forced to fight to keep my status as mentally ill?

You must admit I might be in shock and am justified in demanding explanations. After all, you called me a murderer. As far as I remember, I haven't killed anyone.

My voices confirm, saying:

"Not yet..."

Ugh, maybe I should stop quoting those bastards (one just said: "Please do!"), because I can already see the headlines: "Screwed by his own voices" or "Can voice testimony be court evidence in the era of possible third-kind contacts?"

Please give a clear explanation — why are you accusing me of murder?

H.K.

Email: From w.pawsli@... to hubert.lawla@...

I had decided not to write to you anymore, but unfortunately, certain circumstances are forcing me to do so again. I read your first emails and came across a sentence saying you would add a detailed user manual for the dog. I still haven't received it. Please tell me, who trained that animal?

During my last walk — yes, you read that right — during my last walk with the dog... I'll pause to clarify — I haven't suddenly grown fond of this Gremlin, and it's not like I'm taking him for walks because he's great or anything... I just haven't had time to get rid of the creature. I'm busy writing an important scientific article and preparing for a symposium. Running around shelters and trying to foist this strange natural creation on someone was futile because the dog turned out to be a pretty clever — I have to admit — creature, and when faced with the threat of becoming a stray, he started behaving like my long-time beloved pet, looking at me affectionately and radiating his belonging to me.

I was called a heartless monster. I brought the creature home and, of course, everything went back to normal — the dog claimed my sofa or armchair... Let me explain: it depends on where I want to sit. The animal watches me closely, and the moment I want to sit on the sofa, it jumps on it before me; when I want to rest in the armchair — it squeezes in there, growling, barking, and baring its little teeth. This time the dog claimed the armchair and shot me medusa-like looks from there.

Honestly, sometimes I'm afraid it will bite me at night while I sleep. I lock myself in the bedroom because the dog can open doors.

I think I lost the thread. Take this dog — you'll have plenty to write about. Responsibility isn't necessary — the dog can take care of itself.

What was I supposed to write about? The walk.

So, I went for a walk with it. Usually, he bolts toward the museums, and when I try to change the route, he stops and starts whining as if I'm beating him or hurting him. People then stop and look at me like I'm the biggest jerk. It's a really unpleasant feeling. So usually I give up and let him lead me to the museum, gallery, or wherever he decides to pee that day. I have to change the walk times because the city guards keep an eye on me.

I'm a goldmine for them — I've already paid several fines.

So I went out for a walk with the dog... and this time he starts trotting a different route. And on top of that, he pees on a lamppost! I must admit, at that moment, I was happier than when I passed my first exam at university. I felt like a young god!

Finally, the dog stopped acting out, I thought — he forgot the psychopath's training — happily thinking I'd soon get rid of the creature, maybe by tricking some pampered patient under the guise of therapy. (Yes, I'm creative and have a few plans to get rid of the monster). So I was basking in happiness and even decided to pet the dog. It growled a warning, and the spell was broken.

The dog was up to something.
 He paused for a moment, started sniffing the air, then pulled me toward the cathedral. I began to get scared. Museums are one thing, but if the animal decides to start peeing on churches, I could be in serious trouble. However, the dog passed the cathedral and started pulling toward the nearby park. It was empty — or at least, that's what I thought.

I let the dog off the leash and watched with some scientific interest to see what would happen next. Besides, why am I even telling you this? Trying to reason with a cold psychopath? And why am I sending these emails?

Email: From w.pawsl'i@... to hubert.l'awl'a@...

I kindly inform you that the previous email was sent by mistake. I intended to delete it, but accidentally pressed the "send" button and my ramblings went out into the virtual world.

I'm sure it will give you a lot of unhealthy joy. So please be aware that normal people have emotions — something you probably know very little about.

Email: From hubert.lʹawlʹa@... to w.pawslʹi@...

I read your ramblings with a certain degree of empathy. Unfortunately, the dog's instruction manual, written years ago in case of sudden death by my hypochondriac aunt, is currently in police custody. The officers are going through all my aunt's papers and trash, looking for some clue.
  The investigation is dragging, and I am outside the circle of suspects... actually, there is no circle of suspects at all.
  Please describe the dog's behavior. My aunt read me the instruction manual several times during phone calls, mixing the commands and rules with cooking recipes involving a lot of garlic.
  Hubert Kawka

Email: From w.pawsľi@... to hubert.ľawľa@...

So the police know you exist? You're really lucky I'm busy preparing for a symposium.

Email: From hubert.ľawľa@... to w.pawsľi@...

Please stop copying articles from foreign press. It will definitely come out someday!

Email: From w.pawsľi@... to hubert.ľawľa@...

Unlike you, I am capable of scientifically diagnosing phenomena that concern you. Alien attacks are usually nothing more than a problem with dopamine secretion (although in your case, mental underdevelopment must also be considered). I am smart enough to write scientific articles myself. The nurse you mentioned before is lying about that.

Email: From hubert.ľawľa@... to w.pawsľi@...

I'm so smart that I can't handle a little dog :p

Email: From w.pawsľi@... to hubert.ľawľa@...

It's interesting how you would handle a situation like this. It turned out the park wasn't empty.

About six women of working age were strolling there, and each of them wore the same perfume from a well-known brand. The dog ran between them, inhaled the scent, and sneezed loudly. The ladies started laughing at him, unaware of the danger.

Apparently, the dog doesn't like being laughed at, because he flew into a rage. Here he bit a calf, there he tore an expensive dress to shreds... In short — it would have been the moment of my bankruptcy when the ladies calculated the physical and psychological damages, shrieking like Warsaw street vendors from pre-occupation times. The dog wouldn't calm down, and I had to start repeating, "good boy... good boy..."

Apparently, he likes being flattered because after those words, he stops committing offenses.

Unfortunately, the women thought I was praising him for his wicked deeds and that I had deliberately set the animal on them. The police were called. Due to an oversight, I don't have the beast's vaccination booklet. I had to pay a heavy fine, though it was only 10% of the ladies' demands. Half of the victims took legal action.

Since that day, the dog attacks every woman wearing the mentioned perfume.

And what does the deceased advise on this? Was she perhaps mauled?

Email: From hubert.l′awl′a@... to w.pawsl′i@...

I'm sorry, during phone calls with my aunt I was usually playing poker with friends, so my wild laughter when I had bad cards was justified by the phone conversation.

I might remember something once you review my novel. To make it clear that I'm sending purely literary fiction, I'm attaching a story that is absurd enough to prove that.

Hubert Kawka

Email: From w.pawsl′i@... to hubert.l′awl′a@...

You've come up with a clever trick, I must admit.

First, you send a story where the main character is named Cyril, and then some Cyril shows up about renting a room (I never posted any rental ad).

You probably think I'll react like your kind and start reading signs from these coincidences, like the end of the world is near or hordes of aliens are coming.

Well, you've wasted your effort. As a rational person, I can distinguish coincidences, fate, and hokum from the planned actions of a mentally ill person.

How much money did you spend to arrange this visit? Did I really get under your skin so much in the hospital?

Don't you realize these illnesses need treatment?

Email: From hubert.ɾawlɾa@... to w.pawslɾi@...

If you believe someone is persecuting you, please report it to the police. I declare I have nothing to do with any Cyrils in your reality. I am not renting anyone to spy on you, I haven't trained a dog, I don't know the mayor, and frankly, I don't know what this is about.

Please do not write to me anymore.

Hubert Kawka

Email: From w.pawsl′i@... to hubert.l′awl′a@...

What? Don't write to me??? This is my business, you are the one writing nonsense to me and harassing me. My empathy and patience have run out. I'm going to the police.

Email: From hubert.l′awl′a@... to w.pawsl′i@...

Three weeks have passed, and there is no sign of the police you promised. Could it be that the symposium turned out to be more important after all?

Email: from w.pawsl′i@... to leon.l′rol@...

Hello,
 sorry for not replying earlier to your email. The patient I once warned you about, according to the police, does not appear in the population register.
 The officers suggested blocking the person who sends me emails.
 However, this does not solve the issue of their identity.
 The emails received so far do not qualify as

criminal threats or anything similar, so the police can't do anything about it.

I would block this person, but I'm afraid they will continue scheming. So far, they keep informing me about the progress of their mania.

Could you write a bit more about Hubert Kawka and my namesake Włodzimierz Pawski?

Sincerely,
W. Pawski

Email: from leon.krol@... to w.pawski@...

Dear Sir,

I understand that after my first impulsive response, you might have hesitated to send another message.

There are already legends here about Hubert and Włodek, and I don't really know what it's about myself. I will try to contact the local police; they should have some rational reports. It may take some time to get access as I am busy with the upcoming elections.

I just had a good idea. I think that a definitive solution to the case of Włodek and Hubert will bring me votes in the upcoming elections. People are afraid to enter the forest, no one wants the forester job. The forest is getting wild, and the game population has grown beyond normal. This is bad for the ecosystem and causes losses for the municipality. Yes, I will definitely take care of this matter and ask for your cooperation.

Leon Król

Email: From hubert.ľawľa@... to w.pawslʹi@...

As an amateur coincidence hunter, I was fascinated by the convergence of events involving you and decided to conduct a small experiment.
  I'm sending another story. Please inform me if you encounter any of the characters presented (this could be very interesting).

Regards,
 The Treated Patient

Email: From w.pawslʹi@... to hubert.ľawľa@...

How much did it cost you to stage the fight between the road roller operators? The matter will surely get publicity since a piece of my street was destroyed due to their criminal actions. This definitely won't go unnoticed. I added my two cents and told a journalist about you, showing her the story as well. If I were you, I'd be running away somewhere to Easter Island by now (I think the local community would deal with you quickly there).

I eagerly await your failure.

The Doctor

Email: From hubert.l'awl'a@... to w.pawsl'i@...

This is getting funny! I see that my galloping graphomania can influence someone's life—in a rather unexpected and unintended way, but still.

Today I will write about soups. I think this topic is harmless enough that I can safely write about it and you can then tell the journalists. I am in the process of creating a culinary recipe series called "Kamikaze." After eating it, courage enters the person, and nothing is scary anymore, even autumn melancholy disappears without a trace.

It makes you want to live, and at the same time, death is no longer frightening. An army that bought my recipes would be guaranteed victory.

In a certain book, I came across a character's musings on how the British army might have conquered the world in the past by feeding their soldiers their cuisine. Here's a real-life situation: I was cooking an English breakfast, starting with

frying English sausages. Neighbors, smelling it and thinking I was cooking a dish from my homeland, commented:
 "Smells like shit!"

So I had some satisfaction that they summarized their culinary products that way, but unfortunately, I had no time or place to share this.
 I'm finishing now because I have to check if I can put the soup in the fridge yet, or maybe my messaging session will expire—I don't want to write it again.

Best regards, and I hope a potato from the soup won't attack you.

Hubert Kawka

Email: from w.pawsl´i@... to leon.l´rol@...

Hello,
 Sorry to rush you — have you learned anything yet regarding the two individuals we recently discussed? One of them, using words from your Journal, is "annoying beyond the normative measure." If I weren't a committed rationalist, I would have gone crazy long ago. He must have some otherworldly funds — this might be a useful clue for you and the police. Whatever he sends me, whether it's an email or a story, there is a

rather strange coincidence of events connected with the reality he describes.

Recently, he wrote some psychopathic nonsense about soups and death — yes, you read that right — soups and death.

The next day, an entire locked ward got poisoned by soup. The patients were transferred for observation to the infectious diseases ward, from which most escaped, as I predicted. The disease is unknown. I seriously suspect that Hubert Kawka is involved in the soup incident and now all these germs may spread throughout the city, the country, or continents.

I would share my concerns with the press, but I was discouraged by a press note. I quote it because, due to its short length, it was not posted online on the newspaper's website:

"Who treats us?

While collecting witness accounts of the fight between road roller operators, a respected psychiatrist came forward. We are not disclosing personal details yet, but will investigate this matter. The doctor claimed that the fight was a hoax, staged by a patient who alleges he was treated by this doctor. The doctor firmly denied ever treating that patient. He said he has been harassed by him for over a year.

This information sounded so unbelievable that

we asked a forensic medical expert for an opinion.

Typical paranoid schizophrenia — the doctor, who requested anonymity, stated. Other doctors did not want to speak against a colleague.

"He is a serious person," said one of the interviewees. "If he says something, he surely has evidence. (...)""

I will not quote further as I fear a stroke. Have you obtained access to police reports yet? I eagerly await your reply.

Włodzimierz Pawski

Email: from w.pawsl′i@... to leon.l′rol@...

ov.pll didn't sleep last night and early this morning I came up with an idea to force Hubert Kawka to reveal himself — I'll threaten him that I want to publish his graphomania under my name. It might not be the wisest or most legal idea, but today I received a summons for psychiatric evaluation and time is pressing.

I will keep you updated on the situation.

W.P.

Email: from looser@... to hubert.l′awl′a@...

I assume you have no objection to publishing your prose under my name? After all, you asked me to do so during your hospital stay, explaining your inability to become a public figure.

Of course, we will sign an appropriate contract, consult lawyers, and split the royalties on terms favorable to you.

The Doctor

Email: From hubert.l′awl′a@... to w.pawsl′i@...

I'm sorry, but I anticipated this situation. Attached is an excerpt from an unfinished story.

Attachment No. 1
"Reformed Stomach Lump"
THE TRIAL

The psychiatrist put down the pen, stolen from the reception desk, and sank into bitter reflections.

One floor above, directly above the psychiatrist's room, Artur was creating a masterpiece of 21st-century literary thought, sipping orange tea with cinnamon and cloves, hunted down in a desperate act on eBay after Polish producers refused to sell him this concoction.

The psychiatrist picked up the pen again, which, as if to spite him, had stopped writing. One floor above, Artur filled a Chinese fake Parker pen with ink and continued writing. Ideas came one after another, and sometimes he had to restrain his thoughts to keep up with writing sentences.

Many hours of meditation on the factory production line, where he worked automatically like a small and nimble robot, had bestowed on him brilliance that other writers could only dream of.

That's why the struggling psychiatrist downstairs stole his book and decided to publish it as his own hard-earned work. Unfortunately, Artur, who appeared to be a victim of fate, instead of committing a perfect suicide, took the matter to court and proposed a week-long literary duel.

It must be admitted honestly that the psychiatrist was in deep trouble, as he had not read the entire stolen book, only the first two chapters. Before doing so, he procured a beer stolen from his roommate — planning to pay him back — hoping for decent entertainment reading the patient's nonsense. The beer turned out to be expired.

The roommate realized someone was pilfering his drinks and, in an act of revenge, deliberately put beer with an expiration date several months old into the fridge, which he found at his aunt's, who used it as a "kidney medicine."

After taking several pills stolen from the hospital's first aid kit, which were supposed to induce an altered state of consciousness, the psychiatrist noticed no difference, but his aristocratic stomach did, resulting in a record-breaking sprint to the toilet, jumping over picturesque obstacles like fake Rembrandts given to him by a bipolar patient.

He broke the toilet in the process and, slightly sobering up, calculated the repair costs, then fell into another frenzy. That's when the brilliant idea appeared: to steal Artur's book, make a few bucks, cover the repair costs, and use the rest of the money to move to Malta and open his own practice there (Polish patients were, in his opinion, too dramatic).

The psychiatrist persistently tried to revive the pen by placing it on a hot radiator, but it only ended with a big stain on the carpet.

Email: From w.pawsľi@... to hubert.ľawľa@...

There's no point in arguing with you. I'm sorry you have to struggle with such a severe illness. Please forget about me.

Sincerely,

W.P.

Email: From w.pawsľi@... to hubert.ľawľa@...

Is everything alright with you? You haven't written for several months.

W.P.

Email: From w.pawsl′i@... to hubert.l′awl′a@...
Hello?

Email: From w.pawsl′i@... to hubert.l′awl′a@...
I was accused by the local newspaper of writing emails to myself, including those from you. I would ask you to reveal yourself. It would help me a lot.

Email: From w.pawsl′i@... to hubert.l′awl′a@...
Are you alive?

Email: From w.pawsl′i@... to hubert.l′awl′a@...

Hello?

THE END

www.ingramcontent.com/pod-product-compliance
Lightning Source LLC
Chambersburg PA
CBHW020643130626
46552CB00003B/1375